Stories for Getting Back to Sleep

Maureen,
Sweet dreams

Diane Gillespie

by

DIANE GILLESPIE

Book & cover design:

Vladimir Verano, Third Place Press

Contact the author:

dianemgillespie.com

ISBN: 978-0-9995815-0-6

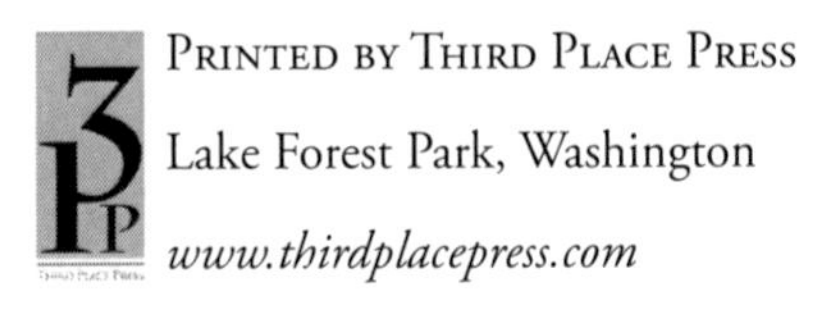

Printed by Third Place Press

Lake Forest Park, Washington

www.thirdplacepress.com

DEDICATION

To all the sleepless people—especially women—
whose good rest we need to create a more caring,
just and peaceful world.

CONTENTS

ACKNOWLEDGMENTS

I owe so much to so many for support and encouragement throughout this project. I am grateful to my long-time writing partner and dear friend Katherine Brown, who steered me through first iterations of these stories and then through their revisions. Her steadfast interest, creative writing abilities and discerning feedback kept me going. I am grateful to Gary Heyde, who was first to hear the whole collection of stories, read to him over several days. He nourished me with his gourmet cooking, attention to details in the stories and thoughtful advice about revisions. I am indebted to Ronnie Thibault, who guided me through part of the publication process with her focused and able web skills; her feedback and persistence were invaluable. I wish to express heartfelt thanks to Libby Cunningham, Leann Fox, Ashley Grolig, Janelle Retka, Bill Seaburg, Gillian Shapiro, Penney Stein, Seana Steffens, Mona Williams, Claire van Wingerden and Sarah Zachs for their insightful comments and thoughtful edits. Thanks also to Vladimir Verano who so deftly led me through the printing process. My family provided love and support all along the way. A special thanks to my husband Michael for reading and commenting on several drafts.

I am grateful to Natasha Newton for her permission to use "The Nightbird Sings His Lullaby" on the cover of this book. See her other amazing work: http://www.natashanewton.com.

I am motivated to sleep well so that I can better contribute to the nonprofit Tostan (Tostan.org). As a volunteer, I have seen first-hand how Tostan's empowering human-rights based education program—offered in communities across West Africa—transforms the world for the better. I will donate profits from this book to help sustain and expand their good work.

WHY SLEEP? WHY NOW?

My Sleep(less) Journey

When I was young, as soon as I lay my head down and closed my eyes, the arms of Morpheus wrapped around me, drawing me in, pulling me close, turning off waking consciousness. As I have aged, sleep's arms have had a harder time finding me, especially after I awaken from a deep sleep because, well, because I need to empty my bladder. Once a night was not so much of a problem. But then it became more frequent. At 3:30 in the morning I found myself listening to relaxing tapes, reading novels, counting sheep, breathing deeply, or imagining restful scenes. A friend told me to give away a large sum of money to organizations that I support until I fell asleep. So many strategies. But most times they didn't work and I found myself frustrated. When my efforts became more dogged, I knew I was going to remain awake. I became anxious, looking at the clock, thinking about whether I could work in a nap the next day or how I could compensate for my lack of sleep. I even took sleep medication off and on for several months, but my doctor would no longer prescribe it, even though I wasn't experiencing the side effects—taking late night drives or eating boxes of chocolates. Without a sleeping aid, I thought that I was doomed to living half awake.

And then I saw the PBS series *Alone in the Wilderness*, the story of Dick Proenneke, who retired at age 50 in 1967 and lived alone in a remote cabin in Alaska. I was mesmerized by Proenneke and watched the series several times. Quite by accident, when I could not go to sleep, I began to imagine myself living alone in Proenneke's cabin. I focused on carrying out the sequence of his routines—snowshoeing, fishing, getting water, cutting wood for the fire, waiting for the plane to land with new supplies, sitting by the fire and then going to bed. I knew he survived and so had no worries about imminent tragedies that might make my heart race or lead me to sit up, wide-eyed and more awake at 4:00 in the morning. Instead—presto—like magic, I fell asleep.

Stepping through Proenneke's sequenced activities became my most reliable way of falling back to sleep. As an educational psychologist and teacher, I've witnessed the power of stories for transforming people's lives. In this book, I am not using the term *story* in its typical literary sense; that is, an account of events with plot, character development, conflict and resolution. Rather I am using the term to describe a sequence of actions that leads to sleep—a *sleep scenario*. Unlike typical short stories, these scenarios are restful. What little tension arises is strategic and always gets resolved purposefully. Proenneke's activities were so different from my ordinary life that I did not start thinking about the usual hobgoblins that kept me awake: the ungraded papers; the exciting new exercise for tomorrow's class; my friend's divorce. Imagining scenarios from Proenneke's life also distracted me from reciting my usual sleepless scenarios: "I can't get back to sleep. I'll never get back to sleep. I'm wide awake. It happens like this every night. I'll be a mess tomorrow."

Gradually, I moved away from Proenneke's cabin in Alaska and its rituals and started creating my own sleeping scenarios. After all, he was a man, isolated and without others in his daily life. What would happen if I created such stories for sleep-deprived women, such as myself, who were in the midst of relationships? As I talked with other women, I discovered that I was not the only woman having difficulty getting enough sleep or getting back to sleep in the early hours of the morning.

Sleep Matters for Well-being

Insomnia, it turns out, is now a widespread phenomenon in the USA and is receiving considerable attention in the medical and media worlds. The ill effects of sleep deprivation have been so well documented by researchers that in 2006 the Institute of Medicine put out a report stating that lack of sleep is an unmet public health problem. The warnings continue to this day. Arianna Huffington's (2016) *The Sleep Revolution: Transforming Your Life One Night at a Time* brought attention to the alarm in a way that connected it to our culture, especially our work environments. She discussed the dangers of not getting enough sleep, explained why everyone in the country needed to think about the effects of sleep deprivation and suggested helpful strategies to help build more sleep into our lives. Reviewing years of scientific research and using his extensive clinical experience, Matthew Walker's (2017) *Why We Sleep:*

Unlocking the Power of Sleep and Dreams further deepened our understanding of why sleep matters for learning and health.

An Internet search leads one to a rich array of popular books and podcasts designed to help people sleep. Remedies and treatments abound. In "A Snooze-Worthy App Collection to Add to the Smartphone" (*The New York Times*, July 6, 2016), Kit Eaton reviewed a new array of sleep-monitoring apps. Pagan Kennedy describes a homemade device that she created herself. It wraps around her head and holds ear buds that allow her to listen to 19th century novels when she wakes up at night ("The Insomnia Machine," *The New York Times*, September 17, 2016). Researchers have found that cognitive behavior therapy for insomnia has promising results (see Roni Caron Robin's "A New Therapy for Insomnia: No More Negative Thoughts," *The New York Times*, August 16, 2016). Insomnia is so differently experienced that no one approach works. Luckily, insomniacs have many options.

How to Use This Book

This slim volume offers one such option: sleep stories or scenarios. Each scenario includes a sequence of actions that results in the character successfully going to sleep. The scenarios are varied by place, types of characters and weather conditions. I recommend that you read the sleep scenarios during the day, choose one or two that you like and that you think will make you sleepy, and read them several times. Once you have the sequence of actions down from one of the stories, you can imagine the scenario when you wake up and want to fall back to sleep, without turning on the light and reading the story. Artificial light disrupts sleep. Of course, you can read the stories during the night and then try them out. But the idea is that the stories are there for you in your memory as soon as you are back in bed in the dark. Before you think of anything else, you remember a story and watch it unfold, like a movie in your mind, in slow motion.

I've found that it's helpful to take deep relaxing breaths before beginning to imagine the sequence of events. Sometimes it's helpful to think that you are pushing off from the world like a swimmer turning and pushing off the side of a pool before beginning a new lap of slow relaxing strokes down a lane. The more you calm your mind before going through the story, the more focused you can be.

For those of you who would like guidance, I have provided tips for working with the stories at the end of each one. (If you find them distracting, skip them.) Some stories focus on relaxing the body, others on how to put worries someplace outside your mind. Many of the stories work through contrast—the main character remembers the cold while becoming warm or tenses her muscles only to relax them. In some the protagonist is alone, in others, with friends. They all have a different way of taking you to sleep—some are about being snowed in, one is about being on a beach and another about sleeping in a tent while camping. Each story starts with the setting secured or being secured so that the character has no worries. Only when secure can you let yourself fully experience warmth, soft sounds, silky textures, comfortable beds, imagined massages and darkness.

The sleep scenes are purposely simple. You can imagine the settings and adapt them to your preferences. Do not insert any of your actual worries in the stories, however. The key is to stay with the sequence—to know what happens next and to know that in the end, the main character falls sleep. And if you drift away from that sequence, think of a soft bell ringing, or wiggle your foot in soft sheets or cup one of your knees with your hands. Whatever action you choose, it should be associated with bringing you back into the sequence. Or go to a new story. Sometimes it might take telling yourself more than one. Following the sequence is what's important. Each story is like taking a peaceful walk through a garden at sunset, toward a cabin or cozy house with a very dim light that reveals a darkened room with a bed full of soft cushions and pillows. One does not even remember falling onto the bed because, well, one is already asleep.

Some men have found these stories interesting and productive for their sleep, but others describe scenarios that are effective for them, sometimes quite different from the ones in this collection. No matter your gender, I wrote these stories because I have seen how important adequate sleep is to the life we want to live and for maintaining the quality of the relationships that we have in our lives. Whether you are caring for children, grandchildren or aging parents, running a business, teaching or working for social justice, sleep matters not only for you but also for all of those with whom you interact.

Sweet dreams.

AT THE BEACH

Sitting in her lounge chair on the white sandy beach, Laura slowly lifted the cap on the baby oil, squeezed some out on her hand and watched as it spread out on her palm. She reached down and rubbed it into her feet and ankles and then, pouring more out, she spread it around her knees. She had meant to bring the SPF 50, but the oil was what she found in her bag. After a clear, hot, sunny day, it was still 80 degrees at 4:30. "Since I've been under the umbrella all day, 20 minutes in the sun won't hurt," she thought to herself as she put the umbrella top down. She poured out more oil and rubbed it into her neck and arms.

About 30 feet from her chair, the white-capped waves rippled through the blue-green sea. The sand on the beach was white; the umbrellas that dotted it were colorful, their awnings fluttering in the wind. She had been dreaming of this exact moment all through December. Omaha had been bitterly cold, the ice and snow keeping her inside for many days. And when she walked across campus to her class, not even her long down coat could keep out the frigid cold. She felt her body tense up as the wind nipped at her face until it felt numb. She remembered thinking as she walked to class that she had never been so cold.

And here she was on winter break, on this beach, oiled and warm. Her family had gone to a nearby amusement park for two days, and she had these days all to herself. Since midafternoon, after a leisurely lunch, she had been reading her mystery, drinking iced chamomile tea and watching some children build sand castles. They shouted as the waves advanced on their fragile structures, as if their voices could push back the ocean. All around were soft sounds—a radio playing music in the distance, several couples laughing or calling out to their children, the waves lapping against the sandy shore.

She watched the children laugh as they raced bravely toward the waves and thought about her own situation back in her office in Omaha several days before coming here. One of her best students had not turned in her last paper, and after much deliberation Laura had given her an incomplete instead of a "D," even though the student hadn't requested one. Technically, she wasn't supposed to award an incomplete without a written request from a student, but she was pretty sure this student would appear at her office door at the beginning of the new semester with an explanation and with the paper. And if she didn't, Laura could change her grade to a "D." She wondered if her students' lives were more complex than when she started teaching or whether they just found her more approachable as she aged.

She deliberately stepped back from that memory, as it started to raise tensions inside her. She thought about the hot sun on her oiled body and then, looking out toward the horizon, she consciously put the memory and its tensions on the sturdy sailboat that was tacking across the large inlet. "Here you go," she thought, "please take these worries with you." The sailors had no notion that they were now carrying her freight. She lay back on her lounge chair and closed her eyes. She took a deep breath and held it and felt the tension in her shoulders relax as she exhaled slowly. The sun felt hot on the front of her legs and arms, and she turned over on her stomach to give her backside some sun. She lifted up a handful of the warm sand and let it sift through her fingers.

"It doesn't get better than this," she thought.

Before she knew it, she was thinking about the three classes she was to teach next quarter and how she would have to prepare, maybe even while she was here for just this short time. "Why don't we get a longer winter break?" she moaned to herself, knowing that the quarter system left teachers no slack. She would pay for taking this trip the first two weeks of next quarter. Again, she found her tensions rising. But she caught herself, saying, "Step back." She raised her head up and looked out and found the sailboat that was already carrying her stress from last quarter. It was farther out now. She sent it the worries for next quarter, hoping it wouldn't go under. She watched it as it sailed, a white feather in the wind, out into the deep blue sea. As it vanished into the distance, she sighed and felt all the tension leave her body.

She put the umbrella back up so that she could get out of the direct sun. Lying back on the lounge chair cushions, she remained present with her body, still feeling warm and relaxed. She closed her eyes and heard a family in the distance packing up and leaving. A couple lay on lounge chairs several yards away; the woman was reading and the man sleeping. The beach was quiet now except for the hypnotic sound of the waves, lapping the shore as the tide came in. She thought that she would read, but found her eyes closing and she drifted off as if she were floating on the warm ocean water.

TIPS FOR WORKING WITH "AT THE BEACH"

- "At the Beach" is a story for those who associate being warm and in the sun with being relaxed. Thinking back on the bitter cold weather at home heightens Laura's experience of warmth and comfort. Remember the cold with her and let your own body shiver and contract and then feel it warm up and loosen in the sun. As you work with this story, take time with each action: Slowly rub the baby oil on your skin; feel the lounge chair cushioning your head, back and legs; hear the waves lapping on the shore; let the sand drift leisurely through your fingers; breathe the fresh salt air.
- The story also has an important strategy for recognizing worries and discarding them. Laura remembers a troubling experience with a student, but she catches herself getting tense and puts her worries on a sailboat, which carries them away. A key for remaining restful is recognizing any new worry and dispensing with it before it takes over your mind.

THE CABIN

Julia drove just a little above the speed limit. She had left her office in Seattle later than she had hoped. On her way back up to her mountain cabin for the weekend, she was trying to beat the first fall storm; it had come in suddenly without much warning. She could see the clouds behind her bringing what the forecasters had warned might be a mix of rain, hail and snow. She had left her cabin mid-morning after an emergency phone call summoned her back to the office, an hour's drive away. Thinking that she had the whole weekend to button up the cabin for winter, Julia had taken off earlier without a thought about what she was leaving behind her. In fact, she now realized that she had left out chair cushions, houseplants, garden tools and her favorite leather gloves. Of most concern, though, was her mother's straw hat, which she remembered putting on the edge of the front porch, easy prey for the wind. Her mother had died a year ago and she found a strange comfort in wearing her hat, especially when she needed to think her way through things, as if her mother were with her there under the hat.

Her cabin in the mountain was small, originally a rickety little place that she had bought at a reduced price. Over the last few years, after she had helped her daughters with their college tuition, she had tightened the place up against the elements—a new roof and siding. Now it was her retreat from a frenzied work life in Seattle. Most days in the city, she worked until 7:00 at night, going home to her apartment carrying the stress from endless meetings, which frequently disturbed her sleep. She had set up the cabin so that on most weekends, she could get caught up not only on her sleep but also on her reflections about life. On Monday mornings, when she drove back to the office from the cabin, she tried to fix the memory of her relaxed and rested body in her head, even as the week's agenda crept into her thinking.

Now, after being in Seattle on a day that she thought would be free from work, she was again driving northeast to the cabin, trying to beat the traffic and the weather. Was that thunder that she heard? So rare in Seattle. She looked into her rearview mirror and saw the storm chasing her. But she knew that she couldn't push the speed limit. She threw on a relaxation tape and, as flute sounds filled the car, she felt her shoulders drop. She drew in a deep breath and exhaled slowly. She tightened her arm muscles and let them relax. The sun was setting, and the dusky light drew her attention away from the fast approaching storm, which she could still see in her rearview mirror.

Forty-five minutes later, when Julia finally pulled up into the darkened driveway, the wind was blowing hard. She pointed her headlights across the front lawn. Sure enough, there in the middle of the yard was the straw hat, which had probably just blown off the front porch. Without thinking twice, she stopped the car, got out and ran to it, swooping it up. She shoved it under her arm to protect it from the first big drops of rain. She got back in the car and drove it under the carport roof, grabbed her briefcase and the sack that held her dinner and opened the cabin door. As she entered, she felt the warmth in the cabin, still left from the day. She hung the hat on its customary hook, sighed a breath of relief, put the briefcase and sack down and headed back out, grabbing the raincoat on the hook by the door.

Once outside, she picked up the chair cushions and her gloves—already a bit damp—took them into the shed and hung them on the pegs so that they would dry. The wind whipped her hair as she opened the shed door; she felt the temperature drop and then the rain let loose. She tucked the plants against the wall on the front porch, probably a losing battle against the colder temperatures coming. Closing the shed doors securely, she glanced around and saw that everything was ready for whatever might come. Now she needed firewood, stored behind the shed. She lifted the tarp, threw a supply of chips and wood into the wheelbarrow and pushed it to the porch near the back door. Her raincoat was now dripping wet, and she felt pellets of ice thumping against her hood. After putting an armload of wood inside, she covered the rest with a tarp on the porch.

As soon as she closed the door behind her, Julia took off her wet clothes and shoes. The cabin still held some warmth, and she slipped into the fluffy dry sweater that hung beneath her mother's hat. She could smell the chicken soup and bread and realized she was starving. She put the soup in the microwave to warm it up. As she waited, she looked at the bed with its warm comforter and decided that she would not light a fire after all, but would wait until morning. She poured herself a glass of sparkling water and tore off a piece of the sourdough bread. Sitting at the small counter, she slowly ate her hot chicken soup, each spoon full of goodies and rich broth. She could hear the storm outside.

As she grew colder, she thought about the delights of her new bed—a mattress top, purchased after sleeping on one in a ritzy hotel; a warm comforter; and tons of pillows. She would burrow down, warm and cozy. The rain seemed gentler now. She opened the back door and saw that it was snowing, the flakes light as down feathers. Listening intently to the sounds and feeling warmed from the soup, she washed up the dishes and filled a hot water bottle for her now cold feet and put on her pajamas. After turning on the bedside lamp, she turned off all other lights. When she pulled the comforter back, she found clean cotton sheets. As she lay down, she slid the hot water bottle to her feet. She settled down, down, down into the mattress, feeling her head, back and legs on the soft sheets. She opened her new mystery, but only read a page because she felt her eyelids drooping. When she turned off the light, it was pitch-black and the wind was blowing through the trees. Ice pattered lightly on the roof. She closed her eyes and drifted slowly into a deep sleep.

TIPS FOR WORKING WITH "THE CABIN"

- This longer story has more events to remember—driving to the cabin before the storm hits; collecting things that could get damaged by the storm; storing them securely; getting wood and food; eating warm soup; using a hot water bottle to warm cold feet. The movement is from outside to inside, from hurried preparation for the storm to increasing relaxation, knowing that all is secured. It's designed for those who want a longer sequence of actions.
- Once you picture the cabin and its surroundings, imagine and then linger on the places where you feel most at ease—perhaps driving in the mountains with relaxing music, fetching and hanging the mother's hat safely on the hook or pouring the hot soup into a bowl. Once the sequence is in place, you can go through the actions automatically, slowing each one down, experiencing each action as it moves into your own body. And remember to ring an imaginary bell if your thoughts stray. Take deep breaths before you start and while you are driving in the car.

THE SPA

Sarah was visiting her friend Anne, who lived on the West Coast in a house with a view of the Cascade Mountains. Anne had convinced Sarah to come because Sarah had been so stressed lately and she needed to get away. Last month, Sarah moved her mother to a retirement home and accepted a promotion at her job. Unlike Anne, she did not have the comfort of a mountain view from her house. Doing such detailed tasks had left Sarah feeling like either a zombie or a bulldozer. Anne promised at least one long visit to what she said was an amazing spa. Sarah's mother was settled, and she had finally completed all the assignments for her last position. Since she had negotiated a week off before going into her new position, she had taken Anne up on her offer.

"How can I resist?" Sarah replied to Anne. "A spa? I've forgotten what relaxed means. Plus, I get to do it with you."

"Oh good," Anne had replied. "We'll rest and get caught up."

Sarah walked into Anne's house and into her arms. They were old friends from college.

"What a joy to see you again," Anne said. "I've told the kids about some of our times in the dorm as college roommates. They are anxious to meet you. But they are out with Harry for the next few hours so that you can unwind from your trip. Let's have some tea. Shall I book the spa tomorrow? Harry's mom can come and take care of the kids."

"Sure," Sarah replied. "It's been ages since I've been to a spa."

The next day after a long morning walk and lunch, Anne and Sarah headed out to the spa.

Anne said, "It shouldn't be too crowded today since it's the middle of the week. They have hot tubs with varying degrees of heat, a traditional sauna, rooms with warmed sand floors covered with canvas and a steam room. Sound inviting? You could also get a massage."

"Yes, it sounds heavenly. I think I can wait on the massage," Sarah replied, feeling the stress from her last month begin to dissipate.

Sarah and Anne walked into the spa, put their clothes into a locker and put on the soft cotton robes they were given when they entered. After showering, they decided to get in the hot tub with the water at body temperature. Sarah stepped down into the pool, easing into bubbling water. Soon Anne was sitting next to her. Sarah put her head back and gently moved her arms and legs through the tepid water, loosening up her body. They didn't talk, letting themselves relax. After sitting for a while, Anne suggested that they go to the 103 degree tub, and Sarah followed willingly. They both gently eased themselves into the warmer water.

"I am a bit dazed from the heat," Sarah said to Anne, who sat across from her. They put their heads back, and Sarah again moved and stretched her body, feeling it limber up.

"This is so delicious," she said to Anne.

After some time, Anne asked Sarah if she wanted to go to the sauna next. Sarah already felt limp, like a rag doll.

She replied, laughing, "Yes. I would follow you anywhere."

Sarah lay down on the top wooden ledge in the sauna while Anne settled in on the lower one. She felt her body loosen more as it dried in the heat. After soaking in the tubs, it felt good to breathe in the dry air. She gently stretched her legs and arms and relaxed her neck and face.

When they had lain quietly for a time, Anne asked, "Shall we move to the steam room?"

"Yes," Sarah said.

In the steam room, they sat on their towels on the wooden ledge. Sarah felt the steam surrounding her body; she put her head up and noticed the faint smells of lavender and eucalyptus. Every muscle in her body relaxed even more. She felt like she was floating. She watched streams of water run down her arms and legs.

"All the toxins are leaving your system," Anne said lightheartedly.

Sarah replied, "Oh good. I'm limp, lazy, drowsy and toxin-free."

"Next, we get you set up in your special sand room all to yourself for a two-hour nap," Anne said. "That way you will be undisturbed. I'll be in the bigger one, which has more people. I don't want you to be awakened by anything."

Inside the small sand room and lying on her back, Sarah felt the heat emanating from the canvas-covered sand into her legs, back, arms, neck and head. The warmth was soothing, relieving any remaining tension in her body. She let her body sink into the warmth and closed her eyes. She turned over onto her stomach and felt the heat on her legs, stomach and chest. She relaxed each part of her body, feeling heat rise into her skin.

She closed her eyes and whispered to herself her gratitude prayer: "I am thankful for my mother and her new living quarters. I am thankful for my new job. I am thankful for Anne. I am thankful for warm sand…"

Sarah couldn't remember the last time she had felt so at peace. She lay motionless on the warm sand, slowly descending into sleep.

TIPS FOR WORKING WITH "THE SPA"

- A quick way to prepare for a nap is to imagine going through a routine at the spa. In addition to hot tubs and saunas, spas now have rooms with sand floors, warmed to various temperatures. The sand is covered with canvas, and people lie on top of it to feel the heat radiating up through their bodies.
- As you imagine going with Sarah and Anne from the hot tubs, to the sauna, to the steam and sand rooms, spend time at each station; there is no hurry. Imagine the way your body feels as you let the heat, steam or water surround your body. Notice smells, such as of the eucalyptus, in the steam room. Take several deep breaths before you enter the spa and then at each station, hold one for several seconds, and then let it out slowly. Expressing gratitude helps you stay focused on what's good in your life.

THE WARM ROCK MASSAGE

Anne lay facedown on the warm massage table. Her massage had been exquisite, her whole body relaxed. Lila was just the best masseuse. Listless after the hour-long massage, Anne checked in with each part of her body, lingering on the muscles—in her feet, her legs, her back, her shoulders, her neck, her head. They were all smoothed out and utterly limp. She was so ready for her nap, a bonus at this spa. You were encouraged to take a nap when the massage was over, after drinking a big glass of water and going to the bathroom. She had just done that and returned to the table, lying face down, feeling the warm blanket below her. She breathed in the faint smell of eucalyptus and lavender, gently inhaling as she relaxed.

"I am so sleepy," Anne said to Lila.

"Good," Lila replied, in her soft honeyed voice, "I will now place some warm weights on you to help you sink into sleep. But first let me put some hot towels on your feet."

Anne felt the warmth permeate her toes and heels and ankles. The towels themselves provided a little weight and she let her feet sink into the mattress.

Lila said, "Now I will place a warmed pad on your neck and shoulders."

Anne felt the soft cloth of the pad; its weight gently pushed on her neck and shoulders. She felt her neck relax first and then her shoulders settled into the mattress.

"Now come the warm rocks," Lila said.

Anne felt the first warm rock on the left side of her spine, right below the pad. She felt the rock's smoothness and warmth and took in a deep breath. Lila pressed on it ever so lightly. She left it there for several minutes. Lila placed the next warm stone on the other side of her spine. She then put two more warm stones, somewhat heavier, further down Anne's spine. Finally, Lila put the last stones on Anne's lower back. The slight pressure from these stones seemed to push Anne down into the mattress. She was so dozy that when the stones, the towels and the shoulder and neck pads were slowly removed and a blanket was put over her, she fell effortlessly into a deep sleep.

TIPS FOR WORKING WITH "THE WARM ROCK MASSAGE"

- This story can be a follow up to "The Spa." If you are still not asleep after going through the sequence at the spa, you can imagine that you have had a massage in a place where people are encouraged to take a nap after the massage. And this massage ends with warm rocks being placed along one's spine.
- The weight and the warmth of the rocks enhance the sensation that many people experience and describe when they are pulled down by exhaustion into sleep—some recall sliding or slipping off into sleep. The rocks help you sink into your nap. Be sure to experience each rock as it is placed along your spine.

THE BLIZZARD

Julia knocked on Jeff's door, anxious to get out of the cool wind and blowing snow, which now blanketed his yard and front porch. When he opened the door, she saw that he had a fire crackling in the living room. It was her birthday night with Jeff. They had known each other since Jeff came out to her in grad school, long before coming out was common. They had remained close friends ever since; she had even been in Jeff and John's wedding. One of the ways that Jeff and Julia honored their friendship was to exchange massages on birthdays. Jeff had perfected his foot massaging skills, actually going to a class to learn all the pressure points; Julia was also a skilled masseuse herself, specializing in head, neck and shoulders. Along with the massage came a gourmet dinner, and she hoped that tonight it included warm soup.

"Did you bring a suitcase for an overnight?" Jeff asked. "The forecast says this might be a blizzard. Of course you can wear my long johns if necessary."

"Hmm," Julia sighed. "I have a kind of emergency pack in my car with basics. I'll be right back." She put her computer bag down. She did not relish the idea of going back out into the cold, especially since she had seen Jeff's blazing fire.

As she walked down the porch stairs, Jeff said, "Hey, John will be home soon; you might make sure that there's room in the driveway for him."

As she walked to the car, she shivered in the biting cold with thick snow now swirling everywhere. She could hear spinning tires on a car as it tried to take off down the block; someone was already getting stuck. She started her car, backing it up; she could feel the tires slipping, but she managed to get it moving and parked it so that there was plenty of room for John's car. As she opened her trunk, she noticed that she could no longer hear the tires spinning, the car freed from its snowy bank. But she then heard, from the other end of the street, the thud and then swoosh of a shovel lifting snow, someone trying to get a head start on clearing a sidewalk. She reached into the trunk and grabbed her emergency bag: toothbrush, nightgown, underwear, sweater, flashlight, water.

When she returned, Jeff was at the door, bringing in umbrellas and shoes from the porch. She stomped her feet on the rug, took off her boots and stepped into the warm, cozy room. Whatever he was cooking smelled of rich spices—garlic, onions, cardamom and a bit of cinnamon. The fire crackled. A bottle of champagne sat in a cooler next to a tray of snacks. On the couch was a pair of wool socks.

Looking over his shoulder as he went toward the kitchen, he said, "John just called to say that electricity has gone out in the north part of the city. I guess I better make sure we're ready here if we have an outage. We survived a three-day outage last year, so we should be good if it goes out. Luckily the stew is cooking on a gas stove." She took off her coat and shoes and put her bag beside the couch. She was just sitting down as close to the fire as she could get when Jeff came back in with a box of candles and a flashlight. "I'm going to go ahead and cut the bread and take the cake out of the pan so that it's ready. The table's set. Sit and relax. I'll be right back to open the champagne."

Sitting back on the couch, she pulled the warm socks onto her bare feet and put them up on the ottoman near the fire. She had had a harried day, but she consciously put aside the challenges by focusing on the flames in the fireplace. The light danced on the bricks and she could feel the heat emanating from the fire. She let herself relax until she heard a car slowly pulling into the driveway, tires spinning.

Soon John was stamping his feet at the door, and as he entered she could see his coat was covered with snow. "Hey, birthday girl, hello," he said. It's so good to see you. It's really something out there. Where's my lover boy?"

"He's getting everything ready in case the electricity goes out," Julia replied. "Aren't we lucky to have all this comfort waiting for us?"

Jeff came bounding in from the kitchen, hugging John, hanging up his coat and playfully brushing snow off his hair as he walked to the fireplace.

"Let me open a little bubbly," Jeff said.

The cork popped, and Jeff filled the glasses.

He said, "I propose a toast to the birthday girl and to the snow storm. Surely all of us will be snowbound here tomorrow and have the day off. Do you want to eat before or after the massage, my dear? Have some of my hummus and pita chips—new hummus recipe. See what you think."

John said, picking up a pita chip to dip, "I'm starving, but I can wait for dinner."

Julia thought a moment and then replied, "Since it looks like I'll be here for the night, let's sit and relax and then eat. We can do the massage after dinner." She bit into a chip laden with hummus. She and John "oohed" and "aahhed" as they both reached for more.

Sitting in front of the fire, they began to unpack their days. John and Julia each told a funny story and soon they were laughing. Jeff said that he had talked to his mother on the phone. She had lost her short-term memory and told him that she was seeing a new man, and when she handed the phone to the new man, it was Jeff's father. They could only laugh at the bittersweet situation.

"But let's eat," said Jeff. "It's Moroccan stew. And a chocolate Italian cream cake for dessert, for the birthday girl."

Just as they got up to move to the dining room the lights went out.

"Oh damn," said John. "It's the electricity gone out, but we have enough heat left in the house and the heat from the fireplace to eat our dinner in the dining room. It's really a big storm."

They could hear the wind blowing outside. Jeff reached for the flashlight and went into the dining room, where he lit candles. John and Julia sat down, and soon Jeff came out with two steaming bowls of the stew. He then brought out his own bowl and a loaf of sourdough French bread.

"This looks so yummy," declared Julia. "I'm so glad to have a birthday party on this wintery night. And I feel so taken care of."

They chatted about work and their families, but found themselves eating rapidly as they felt the house begin to cool.

"Let's have our cake in the living room by the fire," Jeff said as he got up to clear the table.

"I'm so full. I only need a small sliver. I'll have one for breakfast too!" Julia replied.

"OK, Julia. Small it is. You go sit by the fire. John and I will pick this up."

As she stretched back onto the couch, she could feel the heat radiate from the wood now burning more slowly. Soon Jeff came in and put another log on, stirring up the flames again. They were all full and content and looking forward to the cake, which was indeed an artistic creation—layers of chocolate and cream.

"Jeff, you really should think about cooking professionally!" Julia said. Jeff smiled, handing her a sliver.

Soon it was time for the massage. Jeff always started with the neck and shoulders, working down the backbone to the lower back. He argued that relaxation in the feet first needed to start from above. He stood behind Julia, who was sitting on the couch, and started, with his elbow, pushing down on her neck and shoulders. She could feel him loosening the knot in her right shoulder. Her arms fell limply to her sides. "God, you're tight," said Jeff. She felt the day's tensions go, like balloons, up and away. She hadn't realized how tense she had been. And when his thumbs pressed down on both sides of her backbone, she felt her legs relax, just as Jeff had predicted. She could barely move.

Jeff threw a blanket over her and moved to a small stool in front of the ottoman, where she had her feet up. Before dinner, he lit a candle under a small glass bowl so that the massage oil would be warm. He put down a towel under her legs and then took off the wool sock on the right foot. He held her bare foot in his left hand, and with his right hand, he rubbed in the warm oil, starting at her heel. The world floated away as the strokes of his palm and thumbs became the center of her focus. Jeff used just the right amount of pressure in his massages. He moved his thumbs and fingers slowly around her heel and then took more of the warmed oil and moved his hands and fingers into the middle of her foot. They heard ice pecking against the nearby window. John went over to stir the fire and add another log. He put a sweater over Jeff's shoulders since the room was growing chilly.

Jeff worked his way down to her toes and, after massaging each one, slowly made his way back to her ankles and then he massaged her lower legs. Julie sank into her body, realizing that Jeff's touch was sensual, and yet she knew that his attention was not sexual. He put the warm wool sock over the foot that he had just massaged and removed the other one. Without opening her eyes, she shifted slightly, exhaled and settled back into the cushion. She welcomed his attention to her other foot and leg, knowing that she still had half of the massage ahead. She tightened the blanket around her and she relaxed even more into the movements of Jeff's fingers on her foot.

TIPS FOR WORKING WITH "THE BLIZZARD"

- Like "The Cabin," this is a longer story that you will need to read several times. But here, friends secure the setting. Notice the contrasts throughout the story: The warm, cozy house with its aromatic smells contrasts with the raging storm outside. Julia comes in from the cold two times, which heightens the contrast. (You can come in just once if you like.) Also note that the sounds of shoveling and spinning tires contrast with the crackling of the fire and the soft sounds coming from the kitchen, where Jeff is preparing food. Being pampered by a good friend helps Julia unwind, and knowing that she has the next day off enhances her relaxed state.

A RIVER RAFT

Kaylen had taken up Matt's offer immediately—a rafting trip down the Lumber River in North Carolina. She had the day off, the weather was hot and muggy, and leaving Fayetteville for a float down the languid waters was just what she needed. Matt's obsessive compulsiveness was also what she needed—someone who would take care of all the details. They had dated for a while last year, but when seated at the breakfast table, he told her that her silverware didn't match and she realized that she had limits about what she could monitor in her daily life. Somehow through it all, they had remained friends.

She was jazzed about the day. Matt had made the raft himself; it was simple but comfortable, with small chairs, a little table and even a mattress under an area netted to keep out insects during naptime. "Who else," she asked herself, "would think about napping in such a way that one could hear the flies buzzing but not worry about them landing on you?" He also loved to pack a lunch—one that would extend over time—and she was sure the utensils would match. She brought his favorite sparkling waters. He wanted to talk to her, he had said on the phone, about the new love in his life. He didn't want to lose this new woman and wanted Kaylen's advice. "Don't bring up her silverware," she said with a chuckle. "OK, OK," he replied.

Matt had picked her up early and they headed out into the Fayetteville's traffic-filled city streets. When they turned off onto I-95 South, they picked up speed. They stopped in Lumberton for coffee and then headed south on I-74. Matt knew the way into the park and the boat launch. His good friend Brian had agreed to pick them up at the Lumber River Campground and bring them back to the truck. When they got to the dock launch, Matt had Kaylen back the truck down so that he could ease the raft into the river. While Kaylen parked the truck, Matt lifted the supplies that he had unloaded on the dock onto the raft. She joined him on the raft and before long they were heading downstream. This was a section of the river that was perfect for a slow, lazy rafting trip.

"Listen," Kaylen said, "to that birdsong."

"It's the prothonotary warbler," said Matt. "Watch for a yellow flash down low along the reeds."

Her eyes searched along the shore.

"They are an endangered species in Canada," Matt said.

Not finding the yellow flash, Kaylen gazed out at the whole river and its shaded banks. The beauty stunned her—it had been so long since she had been out of the city. And then the yellow flash caught both of their eyes as they watched the Warbler land on a reed.

"A sign," said Matt, "that our day will be a good one."

Shaded by an umbrella neatly attached to her chair, she realized that she was unwinding, more relaxed than she'd been for a long time.

They sat quietly, drifting down the river. She almost fell asleep, lulled by the sound of the water lapping against Matt's oar as he guided the raft downstream.

She woke reluctantly from her reverie when Matt started talking about Janice. Friends had introduced them at a concert. They all loved the band and wound up debriefing it over a late night dinner. For the last six weeks, Matt had been with her on the weekends.

"What's the reservation?" asked Kaylen.

"Well, she seems easily distracted," he replied. "You know, I just think we're going to decide what to do for dinner and then she's talking about the dinner she had the night before with her friend Alice."

"Humm," replied Kaylen. "So it's irritating when she changes the subject?"

"Yeah, you know me. I need things locked into place before I loosen up. It's a paradox."

"So, have you tried to tell her that?" Kaylen replied.

"Not directly. Probably only nonverbally, which I know is not great communication," he said.

"Practice on me," Kaylen replied.

And he did until he had worked out what troubled him and how he could tell Janice in a way that would not be judgmental and open to compromise. "He's really sweet at heart," Kaylen thought to herself.

Matt jumped up and started unloading the cooler to get ready for lunch. Before long, he had everything laid out on the table. It was a feast: bread, hummus, cheese and a broccoli salad. She poured them each a sparkling drink. They slowly ate their lunches, pointing to the occasional fish that jumped or to the moss and ivy in the tree branches hanging over the river's edge. She could tell that they would continue to be good friends; he had loosened up since telling her about Janice. They both lay back as the river carried them downstream. Matt had taken this route before and so knew how to keep them slightly to the left side of the river by dangling his oar. She watched the raft turn slowly with the river. Matt remained awake, but she yawned.

"Go ahead and take a nap," Matt said. "I'll keep us on course." She closed her eyes, feeling a slight rocking motion as she drifted off to sleep.

TIPS FOR WORKING WITH "A RIVER RAFT"

- This nap story includes motion, the gentle rocking of a boat, as well as companionship and good food. Like "The Blizzard," someone else is taking care of safety, securing the setting. Matt navigates the raft down the river and has prepared the supplies. Kaylen contributes by listening empathically to his relationship troubles and appreciating his careful attention to detail. The raft is secure, the day warm and sunny. Kaylen is far away from work and the city. Let yourself imagine being on this raft; experience the gentle motions of the boat in the water.

THE WRITING RETREAT

The snow sled stopped in the center of the village. Karla got out first, took her bags and headed to cabin number five, the one she was in last year. The staff had already started a fire in her cabin, so it was warm. And there was her sandwich for lunch. She suddenly registered her exhaustion from making all the arrangements for getting away for a week. She started the teakettle, and while it was heating she unpacked her bags. Carefully she put out her new writing pen and notebook so that she could start as soon as she finished her lunch.

When she looked up at the clock after filling several pages, she saw that it was 3:50. She capped her pen and got up to put on her down coat, hat and gloves. She saw that it was snowing lightly when she looked out the window. She put on her snowshoes and walked over to the lodge where her friends were gathering. They took off to the north, into the wooded, snow-covered hills. They hiked in silence for the first 20 minutes, but then, breaking the silence, they all spoke to each other, catching up on family and writing projects.

They came back to the lodge, red faced and cold, and unbundled themselves, hanging up their damp coats and hats. They sat in the overstuffed chairs by the fireplace. Karla opened a bottle of sparkling water and someone brought out crackers and cheese. They smelled spices from the soup simmering in the kitchen and homemade bread. They each got their folders, full of writings from the day. Karla started reading aloud her four-page allotment. After she finished, her readers reflected back to her what they heard—some pointed to words that they loved; another did a movie in the mind, focusing especially on images that emerged. And finally, one identified metaphors that had come up for her as Karla read, ones that Karla herself was unaware of. So satisfying, Karla thought, to be listened to so carefully. Susan went next and they repeated the process. And then it was dinnertime—it was a rich vegetable soup packed with black-eyed peas, okra and greens; the bread was whole wheat and still warm. Dessert came after two more readings—an apple crisp. And then the last reader read aloud and they all responded. They all commented that such deep listening and responding was soothing to the soul.

Karla went back to her cabin, stirred up the fire in the little wood stove to take the chill off the room and got ready for bed. She could tell it was going to be a cold night. The wind was whipping small branches against the windows and it was still lightly snowing. As she snuggled into bed, she pulled the comforter up around her shoulders. She thought that she would have the energy to read. Instead she found herself settling down into the mattress thinking of words, words, words, her own and her dear friends'. They wrapped around her head and pulled her down into the pillow like an anchor sinking her into a deep sleep.

TIPS FOR WORKING WITH "THE WRITING RETREAT"

- In this story, Karla is in the company of several women friends, away from daily routines but not away from her creative work. It is the nature of the work that matters here: calming, restorative, joyful. The story asks you to remember a time when you felt deep satisfaction from being creative, perhaps at a workshop, retreat or in your own specially created sanctuary. Contentment with one's accomplishments can produce a deep relaxation that allows for a special kind of sleep. Perhaps it is the knowledge that one will wake up eager to continue on with what one has been doing. Note that Karla feels no pressure to write a certain number of words or to make perfect what she does. She trusts the process, regardless of whether her words come haltingly or with ease.

THE RAINY DAY

Joanie stood at the window, looking out at the rain from her room in the old Victorian house in London, England. She had booked it early because it was central to the places she wanted to visit during her stay. During her first three days she had come into the room at night to collapse, physically exhausted, onto the soft feather bed after walking miles through the city and its museums. When it clouded over the day before, she went to the British Museum and spent several hours with J.M.W. Turner's paintings. *Tintern Abbey* had captured her attention, in part because she could recall from memory a line from Wordsworth's poem written a few miles above the Abbey: "We see into the life of things." And she thought that yes, Turner had seen into the life of this abbey.

Today, she returned from her morning walk, cold and wet. The hot sun that had brightened her first days had disappeared, and last night it had turned downright chilly. After a warm shower, she still felt cold and decided that she needed to take a day off from her sightseeing to rest. A clap of thunder secured her decision. She hung her damp clothes on the shower stall to dry.

As she sat on the window seat looking out through the leaded glass windows, she wrapped her robe closely around her. The slate-gray sky held even darker clouds right above the houses across from hers. Out on the street, people were running—from cars and buses—to get out of the pouring rain. Near the window she could see a small terrace with a wrought iron glass-topped table and chairs. She watched as the raindrops splashed off the glass-top. As the wind blew, rain dripped down the windows. She turned her attention to the features of her cozy room, which she had not paid much attention to until now.

She walked slowly across the thick Persian rug, her feet sinking into the plush. The rust and blue colors were muted by the soft glow of the lamp on the side table, next to the overstuffed chair. She took the throw blanket lying on its back and pulled it over her legs and feet. She settled down in the chair's soft cushions, her chamomile tea on the table beside her. She inhaled the daisy-like smell of the chamomile and the sweet scent of honey. She felt warm now, with dry clothes; her cold wet ones still drying in the shower stall. A small fire was burning in the gas fireplace to the right of her chair. She felt her body relax. All the aches she had from her walks were melting away. Her legs felt as though they were floating; her shoulders drooped to her sides.

As Joanie leaned back in the chair, she noticed the wallpaper, typically Victorian, with small blue flowers on a white background, which stood out against the dark wood moldings. Two paintings of flowers hung midway on the wall—one of the Dog Rose and the other of the Dorset Heath—both flowers with bright pink blooms. She imagined herself lying on the heath in the warm summer sun. She was too tired to pick up the Agatha Christie novel that she had brought. Slowly scanning the cozy room, she felt the tensions in her body vanish. She turned one more time to the window when she heard the gentle tapping of rain and, momentarily, she saw the trees blowing. She closed her eyes and sank into the chair's soft cushions. She pulled the blanket up over her shoulders. Happy to be right where she was, she felt herself slumping further into the chair and into sleep.

TIPS FOR WORKING WITH "THE RAINY DAY"

- Like others in this collection, this story works through contrast: a cold and rainy day and a warm, cozy room. Let your senses linger on the comforting features of the Victorian room—the plush rug, the glowing fire, the soft comforter—and then look out the window to see the rain storm. The story also asks you to remember a time when you were physically exhausted and needed to take an afternoon off to rest. Feel the soft cushions on the chair and let your body relax so that you no longer feel stiffness. A CD or app with rain sounds would be a perfect accompaniment as you reimagine Joanie's experiences lazing in her chair on this rainy day.

PINK SHEETS

Lorna's friend Sandy met her at Chicago's O'Hare airport—such a treat, since Lorna had flown for over 18 hours to Chicago from Bangkok. They had been friends since grade school.

"We are getting Chicago's best pizza tonight and then you can crash," Sandy said as she pulled out onto the highway.

"Sounds heavenly, and better than the pizzas your mom used to pull out of the freezer, I take it?" Lorna asked, smiling.

"I have your room all set up," Sandy said, laughing. "You will be in the small room where my niece comes to spend the night. I got pink, 1,800 thread-count Egyptian cotton sheets for the bed so that she could be 'princess for a night.' We still call it the princess bed even though she quickly abandoned her interest in being a princess. So, tonight you are the princess. It's the small room that I redid after Jimmy left for college."

"I'm afraid I feel more like a worn out Raggedy Ann than a princess, but I'll rally after a shower and the pizza, I'm sure," Lorna said, yawning. "It's cold here, huh?"

Sandy answered, "Yes, and good for sleeping in the princess room. At night, I close it off from the rest of the house and if you want you can open the windows. I have wonderfully warm quilts from my grandmother and a hot water bottle."

Lorna had always been amazed by and appreciative of Sandy's detailed accounts of the world. Really, who knew that thread count reached 1,800? She looked up at the overcast sky, dark gray and full of snow. "Is it supposed to snow?" she asked.

Sandy said, "Yes, we're supposed to get a storm tonight. Aren't you glad you flew in two days early, before you have to go to the all-day meeting downtown? And if we get as much snow as they are predicting, that meeting might need to be put off."

Lorna said, "Well, that would be a drag for our marketing group, but frankly I could use the extra day to recover."

As Sandy drove down the long driveway to the garage behind her house, the snow started falling softly, in big flakes that seemed to stick on contact. By the time they had Lorna's luggage out, snow coated the ground and it was falling faster. Lorna put her mouth up to let the flakes touch her tongue. The cold was such a contrast to the hot, muggy air in Bangkok.

"Better call for the pizza now," Sandy said. "Tomorrow, we'll make snow ice cream."

After a long, hot shower, Lorna threw on her sweatpants and a warm shirt. She could smell the pizza downstairs waiting for her. Sandy had put out guacamole dip, chips and some drinks. They sat together on stools in the kitchen getting caught up on news and reminiscing about their time in high school. When Sandy brought out the pizza, Lorna thought that, indeed, it probably was the best pizza in the world. After her second generous piece, she had only one thing on her mind: the princess bed. Lorna could feel Sandy reading her mind.

She said, "Come on up and let me make sure that you have everything you need."

As they looked out the window, they saw that it was snowing hard. She went to the bathroom, brushed her teeth and slipped on her nightgown. She heard Sandy running the water to fill up the hot water bottle.

Lorna watched as Sandy put extra blankets at the end of the bed. "Well, it might snow into the room and bury you if we open up the window," Sandy said, laughing. The room was indeed cold. Lorna felt sleep pulling her down, her head only bobbing above the gentle current of Sandy's words.

"Aaha, here's your hot water bottle," Sandy said as Lorna slipped into the softest sheets she had ever felt.

"Thank you so much, Sandy," Lorna said, her eyes drooping.

"Sleep tight," Sandy murmured as she closed the door. Lorna pushed the hot water bottle down to the bottom of the bed and put her now cold feet right on it. She felt the warmth radiating through her toes and the soles of her feet. The sheets were, as Sandy said, soft and supple against her body. She snuggled down under all the blankets and turned so that she faced the window. She saw the snow blowing against the faint light of the neighbor's house, blanketing the roof. The whistling wind created scallops of snow on the windowpanes. She thought that she glimpsed patterns, but then her eyes closed and she drifted off to sleep.

TIPS FOR WORKING WITH "PINK SHEETS"

- This blizzard story asks you to imagine a sequence of actions—leaving the snow-covered driveway; entering the house and bedroom; ending with your feet on a hot water bottle in a special bed. Sandy's attention to details matters for Lorna's restfulness because she makes the situation not only secure but also special. Engage your senses. Specifically, focus on the taste and smell of warm pizza, the feel of the softest of sheets and pillowcases, the cool air in the bedroom and the sound of wind whipping around corners of the house. Recall your own relief at having tomorrow's meeting cancelled.

CAMPING

Jamie and Rick hiked down the mountain trail. The sun was setting, and they wanted to get back to the campground before dark. Jamie's legs felt a little wobbly. They had gone up to the lake at the top and gone swimming in the cool crystal-clear water before their lunch. On the way down, they stopped by yet another lake to rest and eat their trail mix. Soon, they spotted the path back to their campground, which was at the end of a field with streams and wildflowers. They saw a few other campers, some still putting up their tents.

It was dusk when they reached their tent. The air had grown cool and they were hungry. Luckily the stack of wood that they had gathered the night before lay waiting for them. They threw it into the pit and started a blazing fire. Rick reached into the back of their car to pull out the cast-iron frying pan and cooler so that he could cook an omelet with all the ingredients Jamie had prepared in the morning. She got out the potatoes and cut them up. The blazing fire warmed them as they worked, and soon, after the flames died down, they watched their dinner frying in the pan. The fire hissed and popped. They leaned back in their camp chairs and Jamie pointed to the stars beginning to shine in the night sky. The smell of pines and fresh air mixed with the smoke and smell of onions, potatoes and peppers. They both said together, smiling, "Life is good." It was an old saying between them, and they more often than not said it at the same time. As they ate their dinner, they watched the shadows of other campers beside their fires and soon they could hear singing, but they were too far away to hear the words.

Rick washed up the plates and pan while Jamie put the food back in the cooler. They had the ingredients for s'mores and put marshmallows on their sticks. Holding them out over the fire, they watched the marshmallows turn light brown. They created their sandwiches, the marshmallows oozing over the melting chocolate and graham crackers. The other campers were quiet now, their fires dying out.

"I can barely move my legs," Jamie said drowsily as she started to unlace her hiking boots. "I can barely keep my eyes open. We must have hiked 10 miles. Not bad for a first day out."

"Listen," said Rick. "Can you hear the stream?"

"It's calling us to sleep now," Lila replied.

"The embers from the fire are mesmerizing," said Rick. "But I'm exhausted too and the cold night air is upon us."

They put out the fire and moved into their tent, zipped up the door, undressed and quickly got into their sleeping bags, which were on soft foam mats. The sweet smelling flannel inside the bags felt warm, having retained the heat from the day. They snuggled down into them and listened to the wind in the trees. The air smelled fresh and the bags were comforting and soft on their legs. Jamie stretched out her legs and let them relax. She shifted her pillow so that it better supported her head. She heard the stream. She wanted to acknowledge the faint burbling by telling Rick how beautiful it sounded, but she couldn't even open her mouth. Before she knew it, she was sound asleep.

TIPS FOR WORKING WITH "CAMPING"

- This story, like "The Rainy Day," asks you to imagine you are fatigued from physical exertion. Jamie and Rick have been hiking all day. Imagine that you are exhausted and hungry, but the experience of being surrounded by the beauty of nature lingers with you. At this moment, nothing is more inviting than a hot meal cooked over an open fire and a tent with still-warm sleeping bags. Open your senses to the smell of burning firewood, the aroma of fried potatoes and the scent of the freshly cleaned flannel lining the sleeping bag. Imagine the darkness, the cooling night air and the quiet of the campground.

THE FAN

Sheila landed in Dakar, Senegal, where it was 85 degrees at 9 p.m. and humid—an abrupt change from her home in Providence, Rhode Island, where the temperature hovered just above freezing. Once she landed in Dakar, she traveled by cab from the airport to the hotel on the ocean. A tall, lithe woman with white hair that framed her face, she had commanded the respect of prospective cab drivers who swirled around her, asking for her business. She had come a day early so that she could rest and swim, something she hadn't done for months. She was excited to see the staff the next day at the nonprofit where she volunteered. Even though she was exhausted from the flight, she was a little charged. This was her fifth trip to Dakar since she had retired. She had served in the Peace Corps in Senegal when she was right out of college and had fallen in love with the people, so coming back to volunteer in retirement seemed ideal. Her husband would join her in two weeks.

When she got into her room, Sheila found that it was hot—really hot. She switched on the overhead fan, which provided some relief, but between the heat and her excitement at being in Dakar, she was awake. After unpacking, she walked over to the small refrigerator, took out a sparkling water and walked to the balcony, opening the door. Sitting on the deck, she listened to the ocean waves lapping against the sandy shore. The full moon created dark shapes on the lawn as the fronds on the palm trees swayed gently in the wind, flapping against each other. She heard the murmur of voices coming from the bar and café next to the hotel. She realized she was hungry and went back to the room to grab the granola bar and apple she had in her purse. She ate outside on the balcony, sitting quietly until she heard the first buzzing of a mosquito. Back in the room with the door closed, she decided on a cold shower.

She stood under the cool water, lathering up the washcloth to scrub away the dirt that she always felt covered her when she took such long flights. Starting with her face and neck, she worked her way down to her toes. She rinsed the soap off and dried herself. After turning down the fan another notch, she untied the mosquito net and watched it swing free from its hoist. She stretched it all around the bed and then, after turning out the light, crawled under it. The mesh netting created a secure tent, the outlines of which she could see from the narrow slit of light coming from the window behind the closed curtains. Leaning back into the pillows, she closed her eyes and listened to the gentle whirling of the fan with its faint rhythmic swoops. If she listened carefully, she could also hear the waves breaking against the sand as the tide rose. She stretched out her legs, her back, her arms and neck, and then relaxed them. She turned on her side and let the fan's soft whirring lull her to sleep.

TIPS FOR WORKING WITH "THE FAN"

- In this story, Sheila first calms herself by listening to the lapping of the waves, the wind blowing through palm trees and the murmuring from people talking at the café down the beach. Inside, the fan provides white noise, a faint repetitive sound at the same intensity. Such a sound can block out other noises that might distract you from going to sleep. Imagine the shower and being clean and cool. Feel the light, soft sheet covering your body. Hear the faint swooshing of the fan and feel the slight breeze it makes on your face and arms.

A LATE NIGHT SWIM

Sheila worked a long day at her volunteer job in the office in Dakar, Senegal. Coming home late, she had gone for a long swim in the ocean and had a sumptuous dinner—the famous Senegalese "ceeb" or *ceebu jen*—a spicy vegetable, rice and fish dish. When she returned to her room, sweating and tired, she turned on the air conditioner. The day's events swirled through her head. She found herself problem solving, thinking about what she would say the next day. She knew, however, that she needed to stop worrying and let the day's work drift out to sea. She was exhausted, still catching up with jet lag, and if she didn't get to sleep she would be useless at the office tomorrow.

❧

Sheila slowly takes down the mosquito net and watches it fall like a silky nightgown around the mattress. As she crawls under the net, she feels the cool air from the air conditioner, its noise providing the background monotony she needs to relax. Leaning back into the pillows, she imagines herself walking out across warm, smooth sand into the ocean and its tide. She dives into the cool water and then floats on her back, letting her body undulate with the movement of waves. Her arms and legs hang loosely, buoyed up by the water. She feels the tensions from the day leave her body. The sun is setting and she inhales the salt air.

As she feels her body lying on the bed, she notices that her arms and legs are lighter, as if they are being held up by water. She imagines the waves rocking her, up and down. Imagining the motion calms her. She pulls the soft sheet up around her neck and shoulders and drops off to sleep.

TIPS FOR WORKING WITH "A LATE NIGHT SWIM"

- In this story, the first part of the story sets the stage and the second is told in present tense. Present tense might help some readers join Sheila in her actions as she falls asleep. Imagine the gentle motion of the falling mosquito net. Once in bed, focus on relaxing your body, as if it is buoyed up, and feel the gentle motion of the waves rocking you to sleep.
- Notice in these last two stories that the main character Sheila drops a mosquito net around the bed. The mosquito net could be a metaphor for a dividing line between the worries from one's daily life and a special worry-free space for sleep. Before the stories can work, one must understand how self-care, in this case getting adequate sleep, is a prerequisite for caring effectively for others. Once one recognizes that one is *worthy of* and has the *right* to this safe space, the more the space can be a source of nurturance and quietude. One can even think about one's worries as getting trapped in the protective net; they can't get in.

DESERT FEET

Inspired by the novel *Wild* and the movie *Tracks*, Jane decided take up her college roommate's offer to hike for a week through the Sahara desert. Lila was working in Casablanca, Morocco, and Jane hadn't seen her in 10 years. Lila had proposed a walk through the Sahara desert last year, but Jane couldn't get away. This time she said, "You're on." A month later, she flew into Casablanca where she and Lila spent two days resting and seeing some sights.

On the third day, they got up early to fly to Zagora, the point of departure for the trek. For the last month, Jane had prepared by walking as much as she could, sometimes up to eight hours a day on the weekend. Lila's friends from work had highly recommended the integrity of Amal, an experienced guide who spoke fluent English and had all necessary equipment, including a camel that would walk with them and carry all the supplies. They had decided to take his weeklong hiking tour through the sand dunes, camping at night under the stars. They would stay in Zagora overnight before flying back to Casablanca the following afternoon. The hike would take place in a very safe part of the Sahara.

After the first day, Jane and Lila found the hiking was relaxing, even meditative. They made it to the top of a sand dune every evening to watch the setting sun. At night around the campfire, the guide was full of information about the habitat and told stories of his adventures crossing this surreal landscape. He told them about the different kinds of dunes and the mysteries surrounding their formation and about the animals that inhabited the Sahara. Over the entire week, they felt well guided, well fed and well informed.

What Jane and Lila hadn't fully appreciated was the toll that walking in sand would take on their feet. They had two kinds of shoes, leather sandals and well-ventilated trail runners, but they both filled up with sand. Amal encouraged them to go barefoot, so part of the time—when the sand wasn't too hot—they did.

By the time they were back in Zagora, they looked down at their dusty, calloused, dry feet in disbelief. But the guide had anticipated their reaction and told them about Fatima, the magician whose oils and herbs brought desert feet back to life. He took them to their hotel where they dropped their dusty bags and called Fatima to confirm that she could take them. He then delivered them to her shop. Although exhausted from their last day of hiking, they were pleased to see Fatima waiting for them in the arched opening of her shop door. Inside the shop entry, decorative tiles adorned the floor. They said goodbye to Amal, thanking him heartily for all that he had done.

Fatima led them through a colorful cloth door into a large windowless white room, cool, moist and filled with a mix of comforting smells—was it some combination of musk, mint and eucalyptus?

Before they could figure it out, she escorted them to comfortable leather chairs against the walls and soon brought over her assistants—Anima and Nadia—who each carried a pumice stone. They started on Lila and Jane's heels. They watched the pumice stone as Anima and Nadia gently scrubbed their calloused feet. They laughed at what a week in the desert could produce—a pile of dry skin. Anima and Nadia left and returned with two big tubs of cool water that smelled like peppermint and tea tree oils.

Fatima came in and said, "Now we will let your feet soak for 15 minutes."

Jane felt herself leaning back into the leather cushions; she watched the water turn a dusty grey. Midway through, Anima and Nadia came over with steaming cups of tea and *harcha*, a Moroccan flatbread, with honey and cheese. As Anima and Nadia rubbed down their legs with soft cloths, Jane and Lila sipped the tea and devoured the flatbread, first with the cheese and then with honey.

Soon, their attendants carried out the cloudy water and came back with tubs of clean warm water.

Fatima was with them, carrying small bottles, and said with a laugh, "These oils remove the smell."

She put in what looked to be baking powder and then added several drops of essential oils.

"Is it lavender and grapefruit?" Lila thought to herself. The question dissipated as she gave into her exhaustion, her energy depleted from so many days of walking in the sun. They needed a long rest.

"My feet feel as if they are coming back, " Lila said yawning. "But this warm water is making me so sleepy." They both closed their eyes and drifted off until Anima and Nadia returned. With steaming damp cloths, they rubbed their legs from the knees down to their feet and toes. Once again, they took out the soaking bowls and came back with more. This time, the water was even warmer and the bowls held cotton bags full of spices, which wafted up to them.

Yawning, Jane said, "Is it chamomile and witch hazel?"

"I think so," Lila replied. "And I smell lavender. I think that I'm drifting off again."

From the other room, Fatima said, "Stay as long as you want."

Anima and Nadia returned with bottles of oil and warm dry towels. They dried their legs and feet and began rubbing one of the oils into their legs, slowly moving down to their feet and toes. Jane and Lila sunk once again into their chairs as they felt the oil and massage. They drifted off, thinking that their feet had never been so happy.

TIPS FOR WORKING WITH "DESERT FEET"

- Although this story is somewhat longer, most of it is devoted to setting up Lila and Jane's experiences in the spa. That sequence is simple—foot soakings in water with various oils mixed in and a foot massage. Imagine that you have never been through a desert and that the experience has opened you to a new part of the world. You are refreshed, but physically tired. Your skin is dry, especially your feet. As you walk into Fatima's spa, feel the cool air and moisture. Note that each foot soaking further relaxes you. Breathe in the different smells that come with the soakings. And then, at the end, imagine the massage with the oils rejuvenating your feet and legs.

THE SLEEPING POD

Sheila arrived in Washington D.C. after a long flight from Dakar. She was already tired after staying up late for her goodbye party the night after she finished her volunteer work. The other volunteers were younger than she, and they wanted to show her the nightlife in Dakar. And an exuberant nightlife it was, with people dancing until the wee morning hours. She had not been able to sleep very well on the plane.

Her brother Jeff picked her up at the airport at 6:30 in the morning.

"I'm sorry, I have to go straight to the office," Jeff said. "But I've reserved one of the sleeping pods for you for 5 hours. You'll love it. When you wake up we can go for an early dinner."

"Sleeping pod?" Sheila replied, dazed and disoriented by the time change.

"Yes," replied Jeff. "They are the new rage. Companies are recognizing that a zombie workforce, burnt out from a lack of sleep, does not create and innovate. So now people can sign up for one of these pods for a nap. I had to trade in my saved up time to get this for you, but I think that you will like it. If you don't, I can try to get off after lunch to take you home."

"Such technology is far from the conditions in the rural villages where I've been volunteering," Sheila said. "But I'm up for sleeping."

When they reached Jeff's workplace, Jeff and Sheila walked to the pod, which was on the floor beneath his office. It was a white tube with a bed inside. Jeff had brought sheets and a blanket, although he had told her she could regulate the temperature.

"It was so hot in Senegal that sleeping in cool air will be a treat," she said. "Even needing a blanket will feel good."

"So there are three buttons inside," Jeff said. "This one regulates the temperature. You might want it to start out by setting it at a warmer temperature so that you warm up and then have it automatically go down, say to 55 degrees after 10 minutes."

"Sounds good," Sheila replied. "Go ahead and set it."

"This second button is for music or white noise or rain," Jeff said. "What sounds good?"

"Soft rain sounds terrific," Sheila said. "I haven't heard rain since I left."

"OK. Just push this button. And now this last button is for motion," Jeff informed her. "Would you like to be gently rocked, feel a slight vibration or feel gentle waves undulating under you? You can even start with one and then program in a change."

"Aahh," Sheila responded. "How about undulating waves for 5 minutes, followed by gentle rocking for 10. And then I'm sure I'll be out."

"It's all set," said Jeff. "Sleep like a baby, sis."

Sheila got into the pod and closed the tube. She welcomed the embrace of the enclosure—a sleep cocoon. It was so quiet and dark. She was surprised at how comforting it was. Lying on her back, she slipped out of her jeans and jacket and spread out the blanket over her. She could feel the heat emanating from the sides, surrounding her with warmth. The sound of a soft rain falling surrounded her. She felt a subtle motion start at her feet, almost undetectable. It rolled gently upward, pushing the mattress up against her calves, upper legs, hips, back and neck. It then started back down again, and she let it roll under her like she was floating on a wave in the ocean. It rippled up and down again several more times and then stopped. The stiffness in her body was gone. She stretched out her legs and arms, relaxing muscles after each stretch.

Slowly, the bed began to move side to side like a hammock. She was being lightly rocked. The motion was almost imperceptible, yet so soothing. She wanted to experience it longer, but her eyes felt heavy—as did her body, which seemed to settle further into the mattress with each rocking motion. She closed her eyes, turned on her side and pulled the warm blanket securely around her shoulders. Before she knew it, she was fast asleep.

TIPS FOR WORKING WITH "THE SLEEPING POD"

- A quick Internet search of sleeping pods reveals many different kinds of compartments now available, frequently purchased by businesses and airports. Cocoon-like structures, many are designed to keep out light and disturbing sounds. Some come with equipment inside that lets you select and adjust calming music or nature tapes, control the temperature and set an alarm. Although many of us will likely not put such a pod in our houses, we can surely imagine using one at an airport or at work. Joining Sheila in the pod allows you to experiment with entering into total darkness, having selected soothing sounds that appeal to you, temperatures that become cooler over time and motions that comfort you as you fall asleep.

NIGHT TRAIN

Sitting at their favorite coffee shop, Joan asked Anita about her recent camping trip. Anita replied, "The hikes were glorious. The getting to sleep and back to sleep were challenging, because at first I thought my air mattress was too thin and that I would need to get another one to put on top of it, and that meant a long trip into town. Instead, I took the opportunity to practice my new strategy for falling asleep."

"Oh really?" Joan replied. "What's that?"

Carol answered, "I use sleep stories, or what I call scenarios—sequences of events—to put myself to sleep these days."

Joan asked, "Can you give me an example?"

"Sure," Carol replied. "I'll tell you my train story. I call it 'Night Train.'"

"Oh great."

"So close your eyes and take two slow, deep breaths," Carol said.

Imagine that you are sitting in a dining car on a train. You finished a delicious late dinner as you and your good friend watched the sunset. The passing lights from the small towns twinkle in the distance. You become aware of the subtle motion of the train and hear its quiet rumble. Somewhere far off, you hear the whistle of another train, 'WOOooOOH WOOooOOH.' You and your friend have each reserved a private berth. You realize that you are very tired, full and relaxed, and that you have nothing in the morning but a lovely late breakfast scheduled in this same dining car.

As you walk to your bedroom, you hear laughter in the seats ahead, and as you pass by, you see a family playing a card game. The person who appears to be the father says, "You've skunked me again!" They must be playing Cribbage, you think to yourself. You glance out the window to see the half-moon hanging in the sky.

At the door of your room, you part with your friend. "Sweet dreams." Entering your room, you admire its snugness: the bed with all its pillows, the tiny toilet and shower. Before you close your curtains, you look again at the moon. It holds the world steady as the countryside whisks past.

Once in bed, you snuggle down under soft sheets and a fluffy blanket. With the light off and curtains closed, it's dark and quiet, except for the slight rumbling of the train on its tracks. It's a gentle sound, the clickity-clack barely perceptible, muffled by the speed of the train. Like a mother's cradle, the train gently sways back and forth, relaxing your whole body. You let go completely. You are carried into a deep, restful sleep by the rhythmic repetitions of the train's lullaby.

TIPS FOR USING "NIGHT TRAIN"

- In this story, you gradually leave the company of others and enter a small, cozy compartment. You have no responsibilities as someone else is in the driver's seat. Let yourself see the dark sky and moon as you close the curtains. Once you're in bed, snuggle down into the warm blankets and focus on the gentle rocking motion of the train. You are soothed as you hear a train whistling, far down the track.

THE BRAZILIAN HAMMOCK

Susan brought in the package that had just been delivered to her house. She thought, "This must be the surprise that Adele was telling me about." Her sister Adele had recently spent two weeks on a retreat in Brazil with a healer, someone she called "the Miracle Man." "While I was in Brazil, I picked up something that will bring a miracle to your life," Adele said. Susan's sister had always been open to spiritual encounters, frequently seeking them out. Not effusive about her motivations, her accounts were always interesting. She never asked Susan to join her, nor did she put pressure on her to approve of her adventures. So Susan had been surprised when Adele said that she sent her something that would bring her a miracle. She opened the package.

☙

As Susan lifts the soft cotton cloth out of its wrapping, she sees that it is intricately crocheted. Unfolding it carefully, a card falls out. On it, Adele has written a message: "May your heart grow and fill with love when you rest in this handmade hammock. I know that it will fit on the old frame that you have in your shed. And yes, it's machine washable and chemical free! Love always, Sis." Susan stretches it out, feeling the soft material and floral designs between the lacey webbing.

"It's beautiful," Susan says aloud.

Walking into the room Carl, her husband, hears her and says, "What's beautiful?"

"Look," Susan replies. "Adele sent us a hammock from Brazil. She thinks it should fit the frame that we have in the shed."

"Let's see," says Carl.

❧

Outside, after moving the frame from the shed, they both hold up one end of the hammock and, smiling at each other, recognize that Adele was right: It's a perfect fit.

"Let's secure it," Carl says.

❧

Thirty minutes later, Susan gets situated in the hammock. She feels her body sink into the cloth. The tension is just right; the woven cloth cradles her without closing in on her. She takes deep breaths and stretches her neck, her arms and her legs, moving slowly until she's nestled in. Her hips, a bit tight from her morning gardening, sink down. She feels as if she is floating. Carl comes by and gently pushes the hammock.

"Rock-a-bye, baby," he whispers in a soothing voice.

Susan feels the gentle rocking. She closes her eyes and lets her body glide rhythmically. The late-afternoon breeze cools the bare skin on her face, arms and legs. Over toward the pond, the birds have begun singing their evening songs. She opens her eyes. A white, fluffy cloud drifts by overhead. The silvery leaves from the birch trees ripple in the wind. The dappled afternoon light falls on her and the hammock. She feels her husband give the hammock another gentle push. Closing her eyes again, she finds herself transported into her sister's miracle--a late afternoon nap.

TIPS FOR WORKING WITH "THE BRAZILIAN HAMMOCK"

- When we bring people we trust close to us, we relax, let our guards down and sleep restfully. Susan trusts her sister and husband; they are thoughtful and attentive to her. Be sure to image people you trust as you reimagine this scenario. Also notice how she falls asleep by relaxing her body, part by part, and is aware of the peacefulness of her natural surroundings—rustling leaves, breezes, drifting clouds and sun. An afternoon nap is a miracle.

THREE RECIPIES FOR SLEEP

The following vignettes are written in present tense. They are meant to be absorbing descriptions of sensual experiences with food that provide comfort through ritualized motion—pouring honey from a dipper, snapping beans, kneading bread. Follow the slow movements involved in these activities until you are thinking of nothing else but the motions, sounds and smells. Let them lull you to sleep.

DRIPPING HONEY ON AFTERNOON TOAST

The glass jar, half full of honey, sits in the afternoon sun on the breakfast-nook table. A wooden dipper rests inside the honey. Sheila watches the sun shine through honey as if the honey is absorbing its rays. She is mesmerized by the golden liquid, uniform in texture and color all the way down to the bottom of the jar. She turns her gaze slowly to the softened butter on the white butter dish and the still-warm, thick slice of whole wheat bread lying on the white plate in front of her. The smell from baking still lingers in the room. She spreads the butter over the slice, noticing the darker flecks of grains embedded in it and the light brown sunflower seeds. She watches as the butter soaks into it.

Sheila reaches for the honey jar, moving it closer, and then she reaches for the dipper. She pulls it out, laden with honey, and moves it slowly over the warm bread. She smells the faint fragrance of clover blossoms, invoking meadows with wildflowers spilling down hills. She watches the honey drip from the dipper, turning it so that only a thin stream drizzles down onto the toast. She guides it across the top of the bread in thin lines until the whole piece of bread is covered. The honey sinks into the bread and butter. She lifts the now-empty dipper into the jar and watches as it sinks back into the honey. She puts the toast up to her mouth, but first inhales the smells of bread and honey—earthy and fragrant, all at once.

SNAPPING GREEN BEANS

Lucy is sitting on her front porch swing on a hot summer afternoon, a pile of fat green beans in a bowl at her side. Her old dog, Posie, has settled next to the porch swing and is already dreaming of her younger days, her legs occasionally jerking. The wooden porch has just been painted blue and the swing white. It's a lazy afternoon, too hot to do anything but snap beans. She and her boyfriend live by a bayou in Louisiana and she has just brought in the first of what looks to be a bountiful harvest of green beans. The smell of the fresh, cool, salty, marsh morning air has long disappeared, and what surrounds Lucy now is heat and humidity. She sweats just a bit, wiping her face occasionally with a handkerchief. Once in a while, the breeze cools her.

She loves coming out on the front porch to do this, even though she could be in her air-conditioned kitchen. Sitting outside settles her mind and brings back memories of snapping beans with her grandmother and talking about what her grammy called "goings on" in their lives.

She picks up the first bean and looks at it, moving her fingers to the far end. She snaps it off; it breaks easily. She smells the earthy scent of the bean as she holds it up to her nose. She hears a light thud in the bowl that she has set out for the ends. She moves to the other end of the bean, snaps it and hears a light plink. Then, she drops the bean into another bowl and hears a thud. Gradually, she picks up the old routine: snap and plink, snap and plink, thud. Pretty soon, there are no plinks from the ends or thuds from the beans, silenced as they are by the ones below them.

She's not hurried. She picks up the next bean, looking full and ripe, and snaps its top and then its bottom. She thinks about the beans steaming in the pot and how she will not overcook them. Her grammy cooked them all day with bacon and some of its grease. She will steam them and drizzle butter over them with a little salt and pepper. As she thinks about the beans and butter, she reaches down and picks up the next bean: snap, snap. And then she does another.

KNEADING BREAD DOUGH

Jill takes a scoop of flour and sprinkles it evenly over the breadboard. She covers her hands in the flour, watching them turn white in the dry dust. The warm bowl with the risen dough sits in front of her. She lifts it out of the bowl onto the board. Gently, she punches it down and begins to shape the dough into a ball. She smells yeast and wheat. Taking the ball of dough, she folds it in half and then buries her hands in it as she turns it slowly upon itself. She takes out a bit more flour, covering the board and her hands. She feels the dough as it becomes more elastic and adds a handful of sunflower seeds. She turns them into the dough, working slowly and steadily.

The heat from the oven surrounds her now; the loaf pans are greased and ready. She kneads in steady rhythmic motions as she looks out the window at the cold drizzle pattering softly against windowpane. She closes her eyes and thinks of nothing but the feel of the dough on her hands, its soft warm texture and the yeasty, nutty wheat smells rising around her. She continues to push into the dough, turning it upon itself and dreaming of a piece of it, freshly buttered, after the loaves have cooled enough to take them out of the pans.

She cuts the dough into two pieces and forms them into loaves. Once the loaves are in the pans, she sets the timer and puts them in the oven. She hears thunder in the distance and moves to the couch in the next room, curling up under a blanket. She watches the rain out the window, and soon the smell of the baking bread wafts around her. She closes her eyes, knowing the timer will awaken her from sleep.

ABOUT THE AUTHOR

DIANE GILLESPIE is Emerita Professor in the Interdisciplinary Arts and Sciences School at the University of Washington Bothell. She has written two academic books and numerous scholarly articles. *Stories for Getting Back to Sleep* is her first venture into self-help fiction. She cares deeply about social justice and volunteers for the nonprofit Tostan (Tostan.org). She lives in Seattle, Washington, with her husband and enjoys spending time with her son, daughter and their families.